Curse of the Pharaoh

by Charlie Branch

The ancient kingdom of Su-Hamut mourned the loss of their Pharaoh. The king, an elder sorcerer of great renown, had discovered the secret to transferring his soul to the next plane.

For thousands of years, lazy rivers snaked through the lost kingdom of Su-Hamut in the land now known as the Sahara Desert. Ruled by a benevolent Pharaoh, the grateful people thanked their gods by building magnificent temples that pointed toward the sky.

As the king aged, his mortality weighed on him, and he desired immortality. He quested the darkest corners of the kingdom to consult with demons and mad wizards for the knowledge he sought. Eventually, he trekked solo into the deep desert to summon the trickster Djnii because those wiley spirits knew the secrets of transcending—for the right price.

Armed with forbidden lore, the king meditated for weeks to prepare for the ceremony. Energized by the exercise, he drew upon the knowledge of Su-Hamut to prepare the first Scroll of the Dead. To meet the ascension needs, he drained the treasury to build a pyramid that would transport his spirit in a golden chariot.

On a moonless night, the king performed a dangerous ritual atop a hidden platform in the temple. Surrounded by lit candles and arcane symbols drawn in blood, he chanted long-dead languages with a distorted voice that crept through the city's corridors. An eerie resonance sent shivers down the spines of those who heard it as shadows danced in the dark alleyways of the temple.

Hearing the unsettling chants, the pharaoh's servants gathered outside his secret chamber. The unholy sounds filled them with dread.

When the chanting finally ended, they hesitated to enter his room because they were unsure what had happened; hours passed until they dared open the door.

On entry, the servants found the king lying in a pool of blood. He was dead. They cried while they prepared their beloved ruler and followed the instructions in the Scroll of the Dead.

They washed his body with sacred oils, wrapped him in fine linen, and placed protection amulets around him. The servants hoped this ritual would ensure his safe passage to the afterlife after they put him in the sarcophagus.

The pharaoh's soul drifted through the veil of this world, through the realm of shadows and spirits into the underworld. The jackal-headed god of the dead, Anubis, stood before him, saying, "Welcome, Pharaoh of Su-Hamut."

Anubis led him to the Hall of Ma'at to weigh his heart against the feather of truth. Thoth (the ibis-headed god of wisdom) recorded the proceedings. The king's heart balanced perfectly with the feather, and Ma'at smiled. "Proceed, noble king," Ma'at said. "You are worthy of the trials ahead."

The king met some gods who helped him navigate the many trials during his descent into the underworld, such as Horus (the falcon-headed god of the sky) and Bastet (the cat-headed goddess of protection).

The path held dangers: Demons lurked in the shadows and challenged the king at every turn. Apep (the serpent of chaos) blocked his path. "You shall not pass, mortal," Apep hissed. "Your soul belongs to me!"

The king held a magical amulet given to him by Isis (the goddess of magic and motherhood) and commanded: "Begone, serpent!" Apep recoiled, defeated by the amulet's power.

Every victory increased the pull of the afterlife. He had to be near the last steps on this long journey. He eventually reached the hall Osiris (god of the afterlife). He sat upon his throne, flanked by the goddesses Isis and Nephthys.

"Pharaoh of Su-Hamut," Osiris said, "You have proven yourself worthy. Prepare to ascend."

The king had done it. After conquering death, he was ready to transcend to the promised land.

After a long dream, the Pharaoh woke up in a strange room filled with chattering. His effort to see the source of the noise was restricted by the burial shrouds he was wrapped in. He was entombed; the well-made bindings held fast, trapping him.

He saw others like him, richly adorned and seated in modern school desks to his right and left. Confusion clouded his mind. What had happened? Where was he?

Voices echoed from the hallway, followed by the click of footsteps. "Imagine figuring out how to cross dimensions, only to send yourself gutted, immortal, and wrapped in rags... the irony," a scratchy voice said.

A deep, bubbly voice added, "There has to be a way to send a message to stop this insanity."

A being of amorphous light entered the room, its form shifting and shimmering. "Today, students, we will discuss the basics of what you call reincarnation," it said. "Congratulations, you made it to level one."

Immerse yourself in the enigmatic world where philosophies, old superstitions, and odd observations collide in **BELIEF SYSTEMS**, our maze, to challenge your perceptions and expand your horizons. Get ready for a mind-bending ride with **FORBIDDEN FUTURES 13**!

SINNERS IN THE HANDS OF AN ANGRY GOD
by Sam Richard

The congregation shrieks in unified prayer within the stone walls of the temple. An ancient building, one borne long before any congregant or their ancestors were alive. Collectively, they wail and gnash their teeth. Some tear their clothes in grief, exasperation, mania, or reverence for The Known God.

All who live know Him.

All who live love Him.

The priest screams from the pulpit, the dossal drapes dripping with their collective moisture behind him. *It is his indifference that we are given. His beautiful, holy indifference. He sees us, but he does not care. Those under the eye of The Known God are in his grasp, not within his thoughts.*

Never within his terrible and awesome thoughts.

The congregants pray louder and harder to match the intensity of their chosen leader. Their parched throats cracked and hoarse under the strain and dehydration. Their bodies are slick with sweat, blood, and tears. All they have to do is continue to pray, but some fall under the strain of it all, dropping unconscious to the stone floor below. Shallow breaths in the pool of viscous pink fluid below the group. Breaths that eventually cease.

With each body that falls, the masses grow louder, both in an attempt to make up for their fallen members and also in reverent celebration of those who've died for The Known God.

May we never know his might, never know his judgment, or never be known to him. May we move through the world as a singular organism of faith and obedience to The Known God. May we know him, but may he never know us. Let us all continue to hold him in our hearts, to fear the power of his might, that we may stand in his powerful and consuming hands and be spared.

The flock cries out as more fall to the floor, taken by the show of their faith.

A piercing cry brings silence to the chapel. A woman holds her eyes in her blood-drenched palms. Dark red fluid pours from the jagged wounds of her gaping sockets. Her piercing screams echo through the great stone halls of the cathedral, threatening to shatter the ornate stained-glass windows depicting the floating building, black skies above, and a sea of serpents below.

Outside the chapel, the violence of her voice carries up to The Known God, and he sees her through the throng of petty, ineffectual worshipers. The Known God sees her and knows her.

The cathedral shifts in his hands, ancient stone crumbling between His fingers, falling endlessly into the eternal expanse below. His worshippers cry manically in terror and anticipation. They cry in failure and self-flagellation.

The chapel's floor splits open, sending half the congregants into the unknown darkness. Before they can land, something meets them. Writhing masses of tentacles catch and devour, coating themselves in the draining fluids of their devotees.

But one writhing limb passes by them, up through the fissure in the floor of the ancient temple. Dripping with purple ooze, the squirming feeler hunts for the eyeless one. What is left of the congregation screams in agony as it moves through them, finding her hunched down behind a broken pew.

She mutters to herself. Broken in body and mind.

The phantom limb gently wraps around her and pulls her through the fracture as the temple shakes and shifts again, the stone wound healing itself.

She is lifted to the heavens, past the spires of the cathedral and their flags of tattered, dusty fabric and desiccated bones. Far beyond what they could ever see from below. Lifted to The Known God. She smells him. She hears him shift and feels the pulse of his rancid breath across her entire body. It worms into the holes where her eyes once were, stinging.

She of such great faith, chosen. They picked the highest apple on the tree out of all of them. The Known God observes her. The Known God knows her. The Known God cares not for her worship.

The tentacle unravels around her, unburdening itself of her weight. She screams as she falls, unsure of what, why, or how any of this is happening. Unsure of what she has done to garner such favor, only for it to be discarded so quickly. The Known God's rancid breath follows, surrounding her in putrescence.

The eyeless one falls and falls and falls before colliding with a rusty spire. It penetrates through the gap in her collarbone, ejecting through the opposite hip. She hits with an echoing crack, and the dark world around her goes out for good.

In the cathedral below, the congregation shriek and pray, grateful to remain unknown.

Cody Goodfellow's
THE USURPER OF DREAMS

THE SMALL GODS OF PEGANA WERE MUCH DISTURBED.

Mortal men and women spurned their altars and forsook soothsayers and priests for some nefarious interloper who had stolen their faith.

In a word, they were dreaming.

Awakening from their once-simple slumber besotted with visions of far shores, lost cities, and fantastical prodigies, the lumpen mortals shunned their toils and went questing for pleasure, adventure, and—most troubling to the small gods—enlightenment. Discontented with the humble fates woven for them by the gods, they threw their lives into the hands of that capricious titan, Chance.

Full wroth was the small gods, for the secret realm of dreams was the sole demesne of those divinities who fed upon mortal worship but trembled at the slightest stirring of MANA-YOOD-SU-SHAI, in the throes of whose epochal slumber after creating the small gods the first and last of gods slept and sleeps yet, all that is or would be forever poised to burst as a bubble with the awakening of MANA-YOOD-SUSHAI.

They took nourishment from prayers but answered them not, and only when they desired to kindle a mortal vessel for their games were dream-visions delivered by the gods. The Usurper of Dreams corrupted foolish mortals to believe themselves, small gods, in their slumber and to unmake earth and heaven, and all that is, or should be, in the dream-sparked yen for some new worlds, some other gods.

For an age did they deliberate, but swiftly upon digestion of this ill omen, they despatch Xun, the Adjudicator of the gods, to quash these noisome emanations at their source.

Long did Xun sojourn among men, seeking the wellspring of evil dreams. Oft was he misled in search of miraculous palaces in the sky or secret seas of liquid crystal in the heart of the Moon, but diligent and resolute was Xun, and by painful turns did he discover by recurring notes in their prattle the occulted temple of Fantos.

The Usurper of Dreams sat astride a humble altar in a vast, vacant hall. Blindfolded, he stared into the veiled netherworld of mortal dreaming through a third eye inscribed upon his brow, from whence a torrent of glistening bubbles was issued. "A Witch-King rises in the south, daring all to vanquish and claim its black-gold crown! An incubus beguiles the women of the Cold Teeth! A cunning afrit vows wishes and woe upon the seeker who frees him from his prison! A fabulous castle in the clouds mocks the nomads of the Salt Sink!" Cackling with delight, Fantos flung his visions into the fallow lands of slumber with a swarm of hands. Taking no notice of the interloper in his court, so frolicked he anon, until his gleaming illusions were burst by the glaive of Xun, that doth unmake all falsehood.

"Cease and be still! O corrupter of sleep, what skills it to bedevil the rest of mortals and turn their hearts and hands from the rightful worship of the true gods of Pegana?"

Far flew the uproarious laughter of Fantos. "By what right do the small gods feast upon the despair of those they misuse in their wanton games?" Conjuring a storm of bubbles like diamond snow, Fantos drowned Xun in dreams. "Let each mortal jest and game as gods, if only in sleep!"

Sorely vexed was Xun by the defiance of Fantos, but not lightly did he strike down the rebellious upstart. When the last stray dream was crushed, and the divine flesh wafted upward as glittering ash, Xun made obeisance to his masters, only to find his mortal blow shook the worlds apart and sundered all that is or ever shall be.

And Xun did awaken upon that altar, which was now a stable for lowly beasts, whereupon he learned he was but a shepherd who had slept while his charges starved, his quest and triumph but another dream sprung from the evil eye of Fantos. In the cities, he learned, millennia had passed, and none knew the names of the small gods nor offered them prayers, but most heretically did they spurn honest labor to contrive instead such tales and crude depictions of their idle dreams, which they called stories and art.

Even now, the dream-man Adjudicator doth seek to slay the Usurper of Dreams, having forgotten that all that is or ever shall be is but a dream of MA-NA-YOOD-SUSAHI, whom none dare awaken.

THE LOST AUTUMN

BY ELIZABETH RAYNE

Surrounded by acres of cornfields, apple trees, and vines that grew heavy with pumpkins and gourds, Asher's was the last phantom farm in Walnut Ridge that had not yet crumbled to dust in the hands of corporate developers. It seemed half-asleep until fallen leaves rustled to the gutters around late September. In the rusty autumn sunlight, something almost began to breathe again as summer gave its dying sigh.

Every year, a pumpkinhead scarecrow stuffed with hay and dry maple leaves was propped up against the barn, an antique pipe between his crudely carved teeth. This gentleman did not quite have a soul but something almost like it. He watched hayrides jauntily ambling through the fields, heard delighted shrieks from haunts after dark, and felt the thrill of children spooking each other and clamoring for cider donuts dusted in powdered sugar and cinnamon.

That spring brought death. Like the others before it, Asher's Farm was razed to the ground, and its land disemboweled for sprawling metal behemoths of office complexes, hotels, and a luxury strip mall, whose windows glared cruelly in the sun like so many eyes. The earth fell into an uneasy slumber as spring faded into summer. That autumn, the scarecrow saw nothing.

The ground Asher once stood on was not alive in the sense that something would be called alive, and yet some semblance of life throbbed from its wounds. Whatever it was that pulsed in the earth's bowels—it knew who corrupted it. When it woke, it came for them.

A threadbare dusk fell over Halloween. It was only close of business on another weekday to the masses of automatons who sauntered out of their offices after five or six. They did not notice the cracks that spiderwebbed across the asphalt of the strip mall parking lot until it yawned into a chasm of darkness so thick the light choked on it. Bodies poured out of stores and restaurants, caving in on themselves, leaving behind masses of crumpled metal swallowed by their own foundations. Before screams could escape the patrons' lips, their eyes, noses, and mouths were carved hollow and raged with flames, like jack-o-lanterns at the mouth of hell.

From the chasm emerged ghosts of long-dead farm bloodlines, Ashers, and others who had been in the dirt so long that they only existed in photographs stained with time. Any corrupted souls who had not already been engulfed by the chasm were snatched by shadow hands that shoved their blazing corpses into shadow mouths contorted with hunger. The ghosts became flesh as Asher's and the rest of the lost farms rose again.

The moon that night was something monstrous. It cast an unearthly glow on the farms and country shops that had risen from gashes left in the ground by the metal beasts. People in everything from waistcoats and bustles to flannels and jeans wandered around, waiting in line for donuts and caramel apples, homemade fudge wrapped in wax paper, and steaming mugs of spiced cider. Hayrides wobbled towards a distant haunt.

On the packed, leaf-strewn earth strolled a pumpkinhead in corduroys and a green velvet jacket smelling faintly of musty cologne, tendrils of smoke contentedly curling from his pipe. He could finally see again.

GOOD KIDS

Erica L. Satifka

story begins on the next page...

They sent us a pretty one this time—much too pretty for this line of work. She saunters into the room with this little satchel in her pink polish-tipped hands, heels clicking-clacking on the tile floor.

There are two kinds of teachers that get tapped to teach the freak class: the old ones near retirement anyway, who are trying to pile up fat paychecks for their grandchildren. The last guy we had fell into this category.

And then there's the ones who've heard the rumors about a classroom full of monsters and think they're gonna be a savior. This type is far rarer, and they seem to decay faster for some reason.

"Good morning, class. I'm Miss Thornton. Let's get ready to learn!" the teacher exclaims with a wide grin. If we couldn't already tell which kind of teacher she is, this would cement it. Her predecessor never wished us a good morning or gave us his last name because what's the point?

Over the course of the day, the change in Miss Thornton is palpable. Her ruddy skin turns sallow and then stretches itself over her cheekbones like mosquito netting. Half of her shiny fingernails have broken off at the quick, and her voice is raspy as if she's suddenly picked up a two-pack-a-day habit. If she was pregnant before, she isn't now, and she never will be again.

We do this without wanting to or even trying. We don't want to be the cause of so much misery. It's just something that happens when we're around.

If the teacher notices the change in her physical condition, she doesn't let on. She continues lecturing until the day ends, and we're loaded into a specially-sealed van and driven back to our boarding house.

Not one of us has a family; they all wasted away years ago. We suppose that's one of the things that makes Miss Thornton want to be here: poor little orphans, poor little freaks.

Scientists don't know what caused us to be this way. They've tested us six ways to Sunday and never figured it out. Perhaps it has something to do with all those microplastics in the ocean. Whatever the cause, a little under one in every ten thousand children of our generation has the ability to inflict indirect harm on others simply by existing.

We can't do it to one another. Hence, why do they keep us cooped up in this so-called school, which is more like a prison with books? In a less enlightened time, we'd all have been burned to a crisp the moment everyone caught on about our differences. But now? Rehabilitation is the goal as if our curse was some kind of learning disability.

How many more teachers will the administration let us ruin before realizing they shouldn't keep sending them to us? How many more people are they going to let us kill?

The next day, Miss Thornton's condition had somewhat improved. It's common for a few hours away from us to reverse some of the changes we make, but the recovery never lasts. Degradation never stops once it starts and always wins.

"Open up your math books to page forty-five," she says in her new creaky-ass voice.

Most of us do as we're told. We're ruining these people's lives; the least we can do is listen to them. But one of us, a pipsqueak of a boy who'd just been identified and placed into our special class a few months ago, raises his hand.

"Can I ask you a question?"

Miss Thornton smiles, her teeth already starting to crumble at the edges. "Go ahead. I'm glad one of you is asking something. You're all so quiet."

"Why are you here?"

Miss Thornton seems to really consider the question. Taps her chin with her broken fingernail. "Because I believe that everyone deserves an education. I believe in all of you, even if nobody else does. I love you all, no matter what the administration says you've all done. You're good kids."

How the fuck should we respond to this? We know she wants us to reciprocate her feelings, but we don't. She's just some idealistic idiot who's throwing her life away to be replaced shortly by another.

We remind ourselves that it's her body, her choice.

In the end, Miss Thornton lasts eighteen days, five months less than the next longest-lived teacher of the freak class. That's how it goes for those who care; she cared a lot.

Miss Thornton's replacement doesn't give us her name, say good morning, or call us good kids. She knows we're not.

It's better this way.

BROTHER RAIN
JAN STRNAD

"Dead," she said. "Dead dirt."

Brother Rain climbed down from the wagon and knelt beside his sister. She crushed the dry clod in her fist. The dirt sifted through her fingers and flew away on the wind, Oklahoma bound. Brother Rain traced a finger in a pattern on the ground, a symbol for sky and four vertical lines beneath it.

"Not dead," Brother Rain said. "Sleeping. All it needs is rain."

Sister shook her head.

"They killed it," she said, "these home-steaders."

She nodded toward the prairie shack in the distance, a crude construction of limestone and wood, abandoned now, a relic in the ruined field.

"It was good soil once. It thrived as it had for untold ages of time, before they ruined it. They deserve no claim on this land. Let the winds take them as it does this poor, ruined earth."

"You're too hard, Sister. They do their best."

"There's an eighth sin, Brother, as deadly as the other seven. It isn't lust or greed or envy that will kill us, but ignorance. I've no sympathy for those who die under their own hand, and no love for those whose ignorant ways?"

"Enough, Sister. I know your mind. This is a time for compassion."

"You're going to help them."

"If they'll have me, I will. I can but offer."

"And again, you'll be disappointed… or worse."

"Disappointment is no reason to abandon hope."

"And hope is no reason to abandon logic."

"Ah, Sister. You wear at me. Come along."

Brother Rain helped his sister to her feet and helped her again as she climbed aboard the cart. She was a tiny thing, frail, almost nothing in Brother's long-fingered hands. He knew to handle her gently, not for pity but out of respect, for of the two, he knew where the true power lay.

The mayor of Prairie Center regarded Brother Rain with a narrow eye. Outside his window on the second floor of the bank and mercantile, he could see the enclosed cart adorned with strange symbols surrounding a beautifully raining cloud. Inside the cloud were the words "Brother Rain" painted in letters stately and clear. The mayor had known so-called rainmakers before, heard their spiels, their mumbo-jumbo, and more excuses than he'd have thought possible when their efforts failed to produce, as they always did. He wondered about the skinny woman who sat on the cart with the reins to the single, shaggy horse held loosely in her hands. She seemed insubstantial, like a thought, or a ghost.

"Guarantee, you say," the mayor said. His tone of voice made his disdain as clear as spring water. "You'll pardon my suspicions."

"I understand," Brother Rain said. He stood before the mayor's desk, his Hardee hat in hand. "To believe that any mortal man could command the heavens, to even entertain such a notion, is practically blasphemous. Yet I stand before you now, as humble a man as you have known, and declare it to be true."

"You can make it rain."

"I can make it rain."

Brother Rain gestured toward the dry fields that stretched to the horizon, visible beyond the homely buildings that made up the main street of Prairie Center. The hotel, the saloons, the dry goods and groceries, feed store, hardware, drug store, tailor, blacksmith, church... worn out, dried out, played out as the population of the town fled west. Only the most stubborn citizens remained, waiting for a miracle.

"I can bring water to those fields," he said. "I can bring them back. I can make them live again."

"And your charge for this service?"

"Fifty dollars."

"More than the average man makes in a month," the mayor said. "Not bad for a day's work."

"A day's work and a lifetime of learning. A bargain, I would say, for the life of a town."

"It's the farmers you should talk to. It's their farms you'd be saving."

"Easier to squeeze water from a stone than a dollar from a farmer," Brother Rain said. "Town is where they spend their money. Dying fields mean a dying town. If this town is to recover, those fields need to produce. What's it to be, Mayor?"

"Look at that sky. Clear from here to the horizon. You expect me to believe you can bring rain when the Lord himself can't summon up a cloud?"

"I expect you to believe the evidence of your own eyes blinking away the rain, your own wet skin, your own clothes soaked through. As I say, the promise is free. You pay only for results."

"Not a dime before."

"Not a dime nor a penny. A bit of ink is all you invest aforehand."

Brother Rain reached into his coat pocket and withdrew a rolled sheet of paper. He placed it on the mayor's desk. The mayor scowled at the paper, He lowered his glasses from his forehead and drew the page closer, spread it out flat.

"What's this?" he said.

"A simple contract in plain language. It states that when I provide rain to this parched land you will pay me fifty dollars cash. It sets forth the date of commencement, the date of completion, and specifies an amount of precipitation within a reasonable range."

"Very businesslike."

"I am a businessman, Mayor, like yourself."

The mayor opened his desk drawer and withdrew a pen. He uncapped it and signed his name with a bold stroke.

"A pen with its own ink," Brother Rain said. "No inkwell required. Quite the invention."

"Yes," the major said. He slid the contract back to Brother Rain. "Will wonders never cease."

Brother Rain recognized the value of a good show. He parked the cart in front of Thompson's Dry Goods at noon the next day. The sun was blazing hot, the sky cloudless.

A crowd formed in the street to observe the ceremony. They gasped and mothers covered the eyes of their children as Brother Rain emerged from the cart wearing nothing but a cloth tied around his loins, his white skin blinding in the brutal sun.

Sister stood in the open rear door and handed Brother Rain the appurtenances of his trade. She anointed his forehead with Abramelin oil. She placed a hawk feather under a headband over his temples. She brought out a statue of seated Buddha and Brother Rain lit the white candle in the statue's open palms. He poured water over a stone from the Temple of Mars, surrounded himself with a ring of fire, chanted in Greek and Latin and a polyglot of Navajo, Kickapoo, and Atakapa. He lit Chinese fireworks and swung a golden censer from India that smelled of sandalwood and myrrh. And then he danced. He danced the steps of the Hopi, the Mojave, and the Pueblos. He danced and spun and chanted until perspiration ran down his face like a waterfall and he collapsed in a heap to the gasps and moans of the crowd.

The crowd's eyes lifted to the sky, and there above them they beheld... the cruel ball of the sun in an unbroken sky.

"Faker," one man said.

"Fraud."

"A joke, like all the rest."

Brother Rain looked at the crowd through eyebrows dripping with sweat. He looked at them one by one, looked them straight in the eye.

"Tonight," he said. His voice was dry with no wind behind it, but they heard.

"What did he mean, 'tonight'?" a boy asked.

"He didn't mean nothing," the father said. "Get on now. That feed ain't going to load itself."

The crowd drifted away like dust.

Sister grasped Brother Rain by the elbow and helped him to his feet. She guided him to the rear of the cart. He climbed up the step and vanished into the welcoming darkness. Sister gathered the props and carried them inside. She closed the door and climbed onto the front of the cart. She picked up the reins, gave them a snap, and drove herself and her brother out of town.

That night, Brother Rain treated himself to half a glass of whiskey. Before taking himself to bed he stepped into the night and looked up at the moon, a sliver of light in a sky resplendent with stars. The night was clear and dry. He placed two fingers to one temple.

"Midnight," he said, and he went inside. That was all it took, but no one pays a poor man fifty dollars for so little effort.

Two hours later, in town and on the farms, people woke to the sweet smell of rain. They rushed to their windows and breathed in the glorious scent. They lifted their faces to the rain and let it wash over them. They rubbed it from their eyes and faces and looked down at their wet hands in disbelief. Some rushed outside, hands uplifted, and danced in the darkness until their flesh goosebumped and sensible spouses ordered them inside before they caught their death. Windows were slammed tight, buckets placed strategically under leaking roofs, and hope returned to hearts that had forgotten why they troubled to beat.

"No," the mayor said. He sat behind his desk beside an open window. Hot, humid air blew in from the street. "I'm not paying you a cent."

Brother Rain frowned. He fingered the brim of his hat while the muscles in his jaw tightened. He placed the hat on his head and pulled the contract from his coat pocket. The mayor waved it away.

"No need to shove that piece of paper in my face," he said. "You're a fraud and you know it."

"I promised rain and I delivered rain. I described where and when and how much. That is what you received."

"What you delivered was a show, and it was a doozy, I'll hand you that. Best one so far and this town has seen plenty. But that's all it was. A show."

"But the rain?"

The mayor leaned forward. He folded his hands and let out a sigh.

"Brother Rain," he said, "we both know what's going on here. You may think we're backwards here on the plains and, hell, you may be right. But we do have the telegraph, and the telegraph tells me that they had a storm over in Kansas City night before last and that the storm was headed our way."

"You knew this when you signed the contract."

"I did not. But I checked and that's what I found out. So you can take your contract and your cart and that stick-insect sister of yours and head on to the next town and try your luck there."

The mayor sat back in his chair to declare the meeting over. Brother Rain did not move for long seconds. He raised his hand to his neck and gave it a rub. He took a long, deep breath and let it out with puffed cheeks.

"Well," he said, "all I can tell you is, you're mistaken. That Kansas City storm was stuck. It wasn't going nowhere. I made it rain here last night. Me. But there's no convincing you of that fact, is there?"

"No, there is not."

"You don't believe a man can make it rain at all, do you?"

"I do not."

Brother Rain shook his head. He put on his hat and gave it a tap.

"Ah, well, that's it, then. We'll be moving on. But if you don't mind, Mayor, I surely could use a hot bath and a square meal. I don't expect you'd object if Sister and I were to check in to that fine hotel of yours for a night or two? We would pay cash."

"It's a free country," the mayor said.

"Obliged," said Brother Rain. He walked slowly toward the door. As he stepped into the hallway he paused. He angled his chin at the mayor's window.

"You'll want to close that window when you leave," he said. "Going to be a wet night. You check that with your telegraph."

The rain beat against the window glass. Brother Rain took a long draw straight from the bottle under Sister's disapproving eye. She sat on the bed, her feet up. She read the Weekly Sentinel. It told of Brother Rain's performance two days before and of a "convenient precipitation" that had blown in from the east.

"They all but call you a fraud," Sister said.

"Hm," Brother Rain said. A lightning bolt struck a quarter mile away. Thunder rattled the window a second later.

It had been raining for two nights and two days straight.

From the second story hotel window, Brother Rain could see the stable across the street. The wagon was safe, the horse dry and warm, but if the street got any muddier it would be impassable. Still, he had to continue.

"What did you tell the mayor?" Sister said.

"Fifty a day, plus the original fifty."

"How long do you think he'll hold out?"

"Another day. Forever. Hard to say."

He walked over and sat on the edge of the bed. He took another swallow of whiskey.

"The problem is," he said, "if the money gets too rich, they'll kill me."

"Go talk to him again. Offer him a deal."

"It's too soon. Have to wait for the river to flood, or threaten to. Maybe tomorrow. No, I spoke too soon! There's a group headed for the mayor's office. Ha! One of 'em just lost a shoe in the mud! They're going to give him hell, I'll wager!"

"What was the last one, Brother? The last town to pay what they owed?"

"Without being forced? Newton. Nice folks in Newton. Honest."

"Newton, that's right. What do you say we go back there, Brother, and settle down? Get a little place with two bedrooms and real beds! Sleeping in that old cart is hard on my bones."

"Can't make a living in one place. Rainmaker's got to keep moving."

"We could do something else. Open a store, maybe. What do you say, Brother? Newton was a fine little town."

"We'll see. Do you want to go downstairs for supper?"

"I'm tired. Does it have to thunder? That lightning is so close."

"Rain comes with thunder and lightning, Sister. That's life."

"I suppose," she said. "I'm tired. I don't want supper. I just want to go to bed."

"I'm going down, then."

"You go on. Maybe… maybe there could be a little break? Just a short one, so I could go to sleep?"

"Maybe a short one," Brother said.

"A man can not make rain," the mayor said.

"If you say so." Brother Rain stirred his beef stew, staring into the thick mixture like a seer into a gazing bowl.

"Any educated man knows it. And yet, here we are. You claiming you can, you claiming you can make it stop. And there's people in this town that believe you."

He shook his head.

"It's a helluva note. All right, then. I'll pay your fifty dollars."

"A hundred and fifty," Brother Rain said. "I told you, the original fifty and fifty a day penalty."

"You're a damned scoundrel!"

Brother Rain pounded the table. The bowl of stew bounced and sloshed. A fork clattered to the floor.

"We had a contract!" he said. "I honored it! I am the injured party here, not you!"

"What's your game? You know when it's going to rain, is that it? You've got a knee that hurts, a bunion that swells up? What exactly is your con, Brother Rain?"

"Everything's a con to your kind."

"Oh? What is my kind, Brother Rain?"

"The takers. The high and mighty who think they own it all. They think because a man comes into town with nothing more than a horse and a cart, they can treat him like trash, cheat him, take advantage because he's somehow lower than them, because they think he has no recourse. But I have recourse, Mr. Mayor. The heavens above are my recourse. I command them! Pay me what you owe me and I'll stop this rain and be on my way, never to return. Or cheat me and watch your precious town washed away like it never existed."

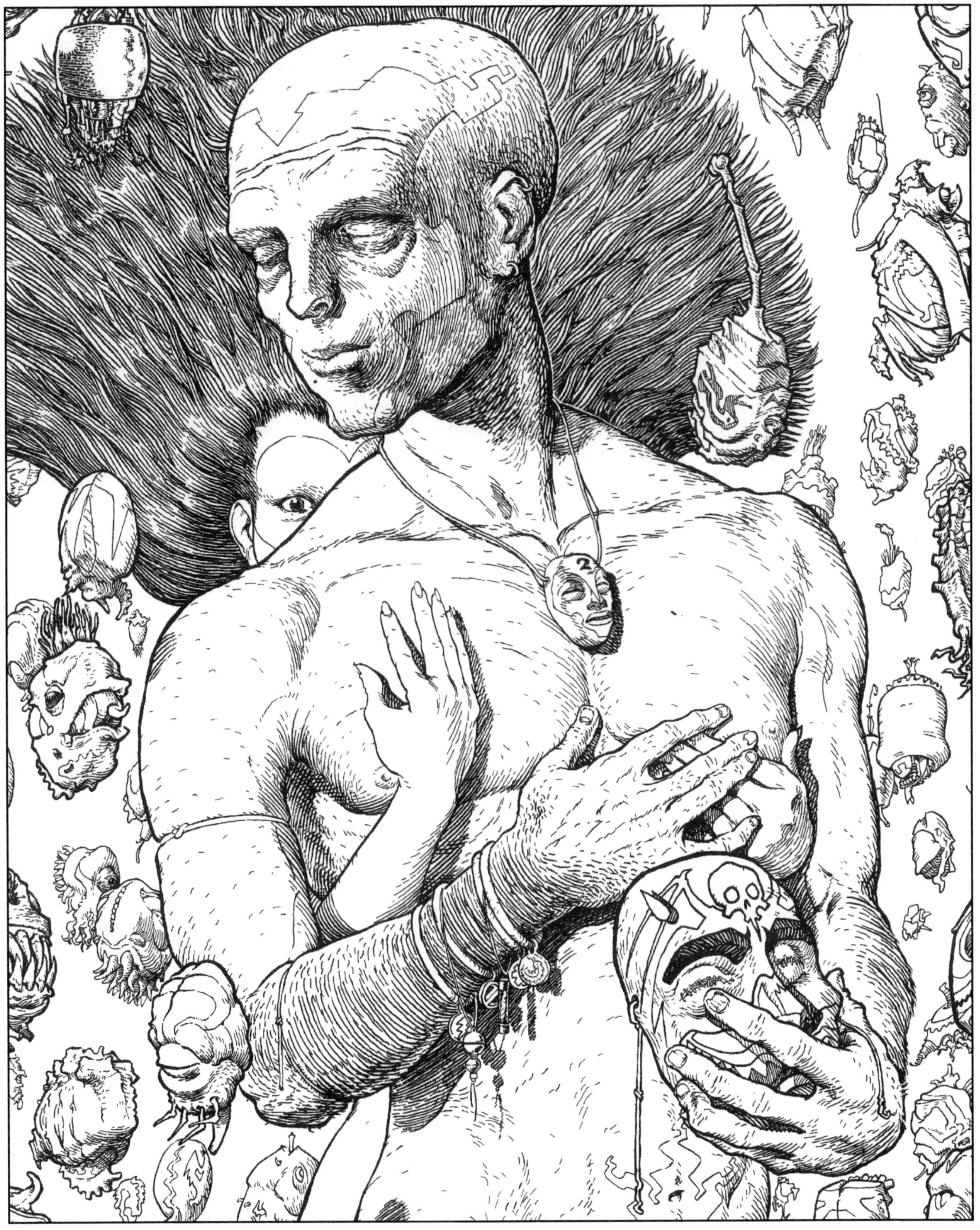

"Seventy-five. That's my last offer."

"One-fifty. Tomorrow it'll be two hundred."

The mayor's jaw worked as he stared at Brother Rain across the table. Brother Rain stared back. The mayor slid his chair back with a squeal. His eyes never left Brother Rain's as he rose.

"We'll see about that," he said.

Brother Rain returned his attention to his stew.

Sister could not sleep. It wasn't the rain and the thunder and lightning. Brother Rain had reduced the storm to a pleasant shower, but there was another storm brewing. It was the storm between Brother and the town of Prairie Center. From Brother's description, the mayor didn't sound like a man who could be intimidated easily. The townspeople were another matter. Too easily intimidated maybe. Too easily frightened, and frightened people form mobs.

When he returned, she would try to talk him into leaving with or without the money. She would try to steer him back to Newton, but if he wanted to press on to Oklahoma and Texas, that would be all right, too. She had a bad feeling about Prairie Center.

Brother Rain needed whiskey. He stepped outside the hotel and paused. The rain fell steadily. It made bubbles where the water gathered in pools. It pattered against his hat and streamed off the brim. The moon, obscured by clouds, did nothing to illuminate his way, but all he needed to do was cross the street to the saloon. He stepped off the boardwalk and into the mud. It sucked at his boots. Each step was an effort but he made his way step by step, drawn to the light that spilled from the open saloon door.

As he gained the boardwalk, they came at him from the darkness of the alley. Four shadowy figures. They smelled of alcohol and sweat and damp. Something hard struck him on the back of the head. His vision swirled and he staggered. The figures pummeled his back, his shoulders, his head, his legs. He fell.

Brother Rain, bathed in the yellow glow from the saloon door, lay on the boardwalk, arms wrapped around his head to shield himself from the fists and boots of his attackers. He felt his mind and his power slipping away.

"Look!" a voice said. "It's stopping!"

The blows ceased. The boots of the shadow men withdrew.

The mayor stepped into the street. He looked up at the parting clouds, the clearing sky, the revealed moon. He smiled, then he walked back to where Brother Rain lay on the boardwalk. He leaned in close, not knowing or caring if the rainmaker was alive or dead.

"Maybe I was wrong about you, Brother Rain," he said. "Maybe you do have a power. At any rate, it's gone now."

"Mayor… the hotel!" a man cried.

The mayor looked in the direction the man pointed. His eyes went to the second story, to the window where the thin woman stood, a silhouette against the light inside.

"She saw."

"Doesn't matter," the mayor said.

Brother Rain moaned. He tried to speak but the words stuck in his throat. The mayor walked over and put his ear to Brother Rain's mouth.

"It matters," Brother Rain said.

In the hotel window, Sister placed two fingers to her temple.

"Midnight," she said.

The cart was far away from Prairie Center when Brother Rain woke. Sister had tended him as well as she could but she hoped there was a doctor in the next town.

"Did you?" Brother Rain asked.

"Oh, yes," Sister said. She dabbed with a damp cloth at the bloody wounds on Brother Rain's face. "Yes. Yes. Yes."

"You didn't need to."

"I did."

"You wear at me, Sister," Brother said. "Sometimes you are… so cruel."

"I know," Sister said.

In Prairie Center at midnight, a stillness descended over the town. Overhead the clouds gathered in a dark shelf. From that shelf a twisting funnel of wind took form, descended, and struck the earth roaring.

BEFORE

AFTER

THE HUNTER
BY PHILIP FRACASSI

WHEN I WAS A BOY, THE BASEMENT WAS MY SANCTUARY.

I'd removed the bulb from the lone socket in that empty concrete room, preferring the dark. The stairs—rotting naked wood but sturdy—could only be illuminated via the open door at the top, leading to a hallway that was murky, even on bright days.

At first, the basement was a hiding place, while above, my father stomped and screamed, hunting for me. Veins thrumming with poison.

Later, it became a dare.

How long could I sit in the dark? Invisible to myself. To him.

Huddled within that perfect black, I became nothing. Ether. Pure spirit.

Even shadows need light to exist.

Without light, Father would not come down. He'd holler from the opening, angry and terrified. A mad dog barking at the void. Below, I'd sit quietly in the center of the cold concrete room, watching the shape of him.

To my father, I was formless; a rogue memory of hate stretched across the basement's expanse, pure as outer space. My eyes, perhaps, pinprick stars.

It was only after several visits to that underground world, that lightless void, that I began to feel the other.

To commune.

The first time, timid fingers pressed at the back of my neck. Cold. Dry.

I gasped but did not move. Could see nothing. Held my breath and ignored my thumping heart as she bushed my cheeks, lightly touched my closed eye-lids, and pressed against my bare knees. An icy hand slid up my shirt, spreading like a starfish against my spine while I took deep breaths of moist, chilled air.

I was not afraid.

Meanwhile, upstairs, my father screamed and beat the floor with footsteps like thunder, his anger a thunderstorm unleashed in hallways and bedrooms and kitchens. After a time, once things calmed in the house above, I'd leave the basement. Slowly, quietly. I'd leave her and return to my bedroom. I'd make a sandwich, steal a Coke, hide behind a flimsy door. I'd play the part of boyhood. The role of Son. And Father would breathe heavy in his own bed, a balustrade of guardianship between cannons of violence.

Days would pass. Weeks.

Often, I'd return to the darkness in the basement. To what waited for me there, eager now, craving my warmth. I'd allow it to do what it wanted while my father hunted. Whisper in my ear, draw on my flesh with pointed fingernails.

As the life above became more ethereal, my life below became an entrapment. A cautious dialogue building toward something more concrete, more binding.

I'd wince and softly cry while she carved herself into my skin, feverishly speaking words of comfort as if both our lives depended on it.

The last time he caught me I'd been asleep in my room.

It was late, and I'd thought myself safe. But he'd kicked in the door, howling. Yanked away my blanket and threw it to the soiled carpet. His large hand clenched my ankle and yanked me off the bed, and my body thumped to the floor. I reached for a hold, for something to save me, as he dragged my body into the tight hall. He strode wordlessly as I panted in terror, sliding against rough wood, naked but for boxers, one size too small.

In the kitchen, peeled lips of chipped linoleum scraped across my back. I winced but did not cry out. Still clutching my leg, eyes wild with delirious need, he searched the drawers for an instrument. Silverware waterfalls crashed to the floor; spatulas and worn wooden spoons clattered. Finally, he pulled out a knife with a black handle, the blade maybe three inches. What you might use to peel an apple.

I jerked free of his grip, flipped over, and began to crawl. Suffocating terror filled my chest and throat. But he was fast—evil things always are—and reached my legs, dropped his weight on the backs of them, trapping me. He stabbed the knife into my left calf and began to cut upward in a vertical line. A black flesh butcher muttering indecipherable words—a language born from needles—as he sawed open my leg, blade chewing through muscle.

I screamed, but the pain, adrenalized, gave me strength. I yanked my other leg free and kicked heel into jaw. He grunted, loosened his hold, and I kicked again, met bony shoulder. I sprang to my feet and ran for the basement, ignoring the burning and bleeding, the damage he'd done.

I yanked open the door and made it one step. He shoved me from behind, and I flew forward into the dark, arms raised in protection. I landed hard on the stairs; ribs and hip bone hit edges, breath punched from my lungs. I scurried like a spider down the last few steps across the cold floor.

"Help me," I panted.

The temperature plummeted as if one of the walls had split like a mouth to reveal an abyssal, web-strewn cave leading to a dark ocean. She emerged and pressed her hungry, ghostly flesh against mine. One long arm wrapped itself around my bare, skinny waist. Her mouth, the only warm part of her, sucked on my ear. Too many teeth nibbled at the edges. Her voice the scrape of rust off metal.

"Promise," she whispered.

I nodded, my body trembling with cold and fear. Blood flowed freely down my burning leg, and I felt my mind weaken. "Yes," I said, knowing what she wanted of me. She'd asked so many times... "Yes."

Father paced the hallway, his restless shadow a fluttering crow's wing through the basement's open door. He mumbled, argued, screamed. All the while

stomping his boots, his petulant anger confused by murderous desire, his twisted brain unknotted by clean thoughts of murder.

"Coward!" I yelled. "Bitch coward!"

He broke like an avalanche, pounding down the stairs as if using six legs instead of two. Inarticulate yelps and barks sounded above beating limbs, his poisonous mouth stuffed with pigs as they were chopped and gutted.

He had just stepped off the last stair onto the concrete when the door above slammed shut, sealing us in with cold finality. Heavy, rapid breathing moved through the dark as he hunted, boots scraped concrete as I slid silently away. I found a corner and tucked into it, made myself small.

As my eyes adjusted, I could make out his form moving side-to-side, arms swiping, feet kicking, hoping to catch flesh.

She whispered something as she let me go and moved in, a spider dancing toward prey. When she wrapped her arms around him, he shrieked into the dark. He cried out for me and begged, the surge of sobriety a terror reflex, an eruption of clarity triggered by the human desire to stay alive.

As he wept and roared, she fed. I watched the dark shadow of his body compress and warp into unnatural angles. A doll made of sticks. The snap of bones was midnight gunshots mixed with the guttural squelch of pressure-split skin; a splash of blood hit the floor as if from an overturned bucket.

Satiated, she came back to me. Icy fingers carved frantically into my flesh. I laid back and spread my arms and legs as she worked.

Hours later, I emerged.

I knotted a kitchen towel around my leg to slow the blood trickle running over my heel. One wound of many.

In the bathroom, I studied my naked body, bathed in hazy yellow.

My palms were no longer creased with lines but concentric circles. Hieroglyphs had been etched into my skin—the inside of my thighs. My back. My neck. My belly.

A promise tattooed into flesh. A contract.

Where I live, there are many fathers like mine.

Fat black flies.

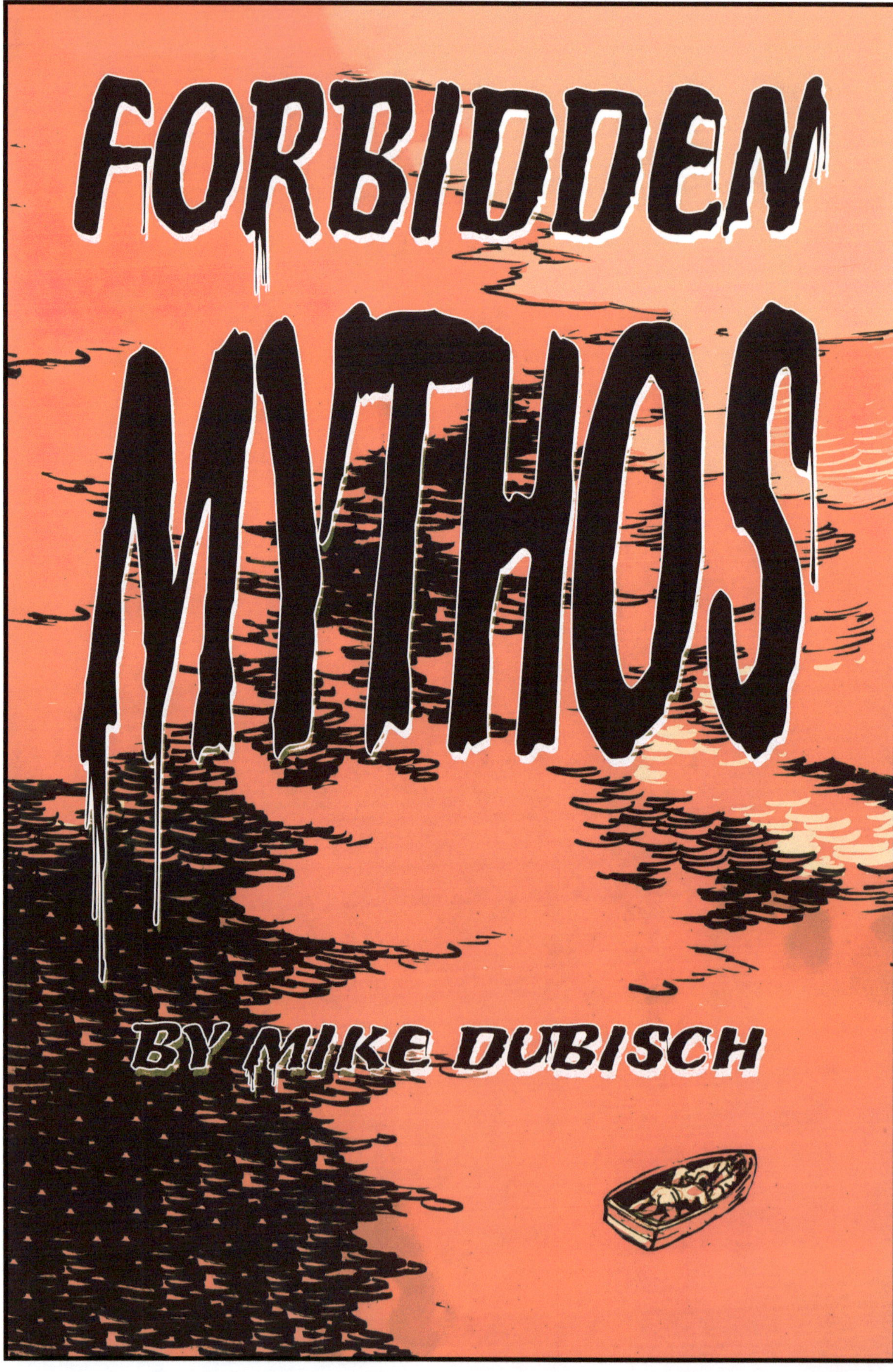
FORBIDDEN MYTHOS
BY MIKE DUBISCH

AYE, AYE, PERVS, IT'S ME COCKTHULHU! PRESENTING ANOTHER DAGON HORRIFYING PIECE OF A TALE—
THESE TWO LOVERS, ADRIFT AT SEA, HIM OFFERING HER WHAT SUSTENANCE HE CAN FROM HIS OWN LOINS— BUT THERE'S NO HAPPY ENDING IN THIS... FORBIDDEN MYTHOS!
ALMOST THERE, BABY....
SHLUP!

UHHHHH....

SO GOOD....

LOOK THERE, AN ISLAND!
IT'S NASTY! IT'S ALL DEAD FISH AND CORAL!
WHAT THE FUCK IS THAT?
SOME SORT OF OBELISK!
BUT WHO ERECTED IT? AND WHY?

LOOK, THERE ARE SOME SORT OF GLYPHS CARVED INTO THE SCALES!

FISH PEOPLE?

WHAT DOES IT MEAN?

I DON'T KNOW.

CHRIS, I'M AFRAID!

TESS... WE'LL REST NOW. WE SHOULD BE SAFE HERE.

WE'LL TRY TO FIND FOOD IN THE MORNING. I'M STILL AS GOOD AS BEFORE. TESS, BABY...

TESS?

TESS, WHERE ARE YOU?

TESS!!!

MMMMMMM....
TESS?
NO-MMMMMMM!

OHHH…

AHHHH…..

SPLOOG!

TESS!!!

FISH-FACED
BASTARDS!
WHAT ARE YOU
DOING?

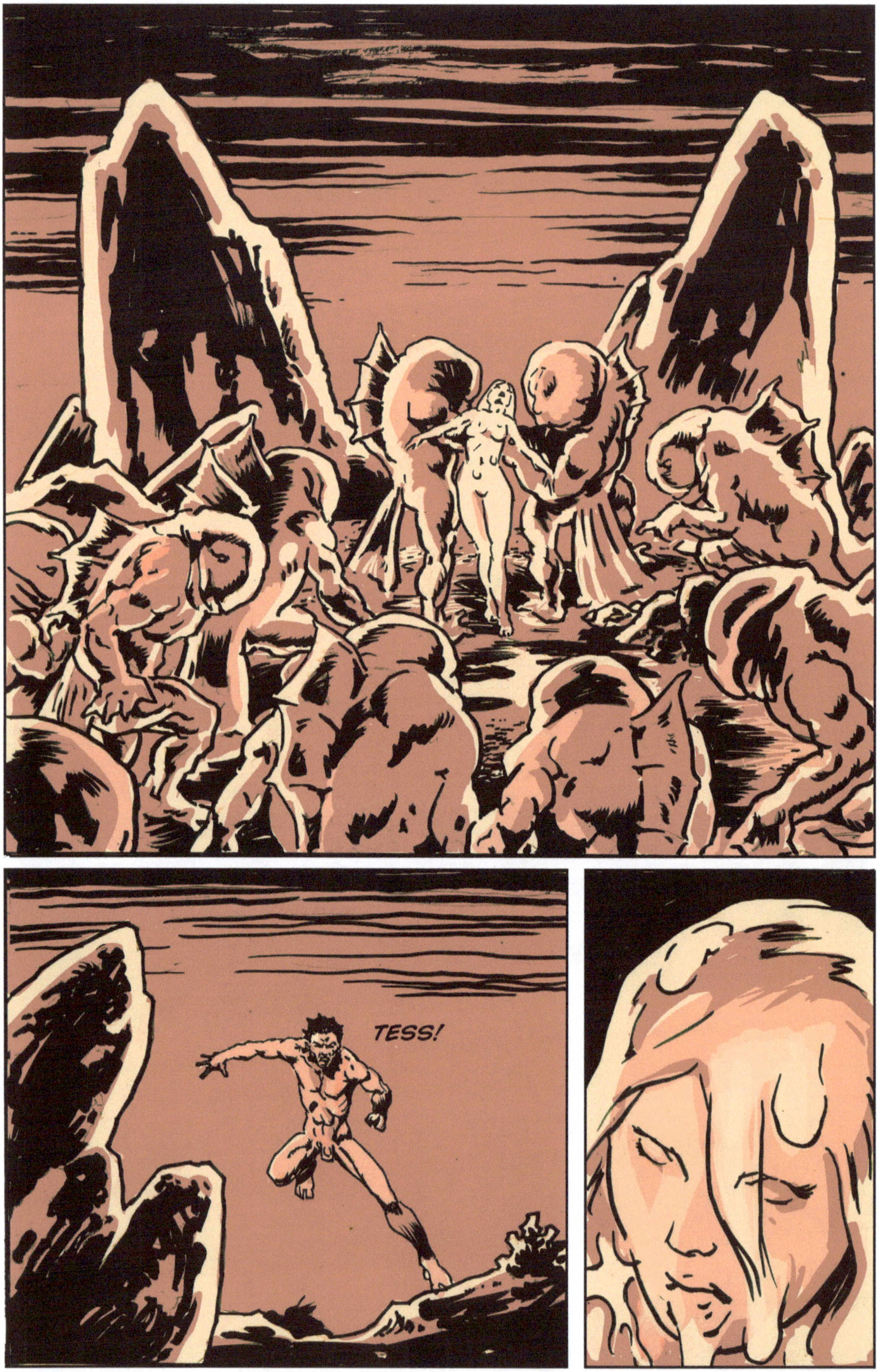

TESS!

MMMMMMMMMM....

MRRRRR....

RRRRRRRRR....

SPLASH!!

TESS, I'LL SAVE YOU!

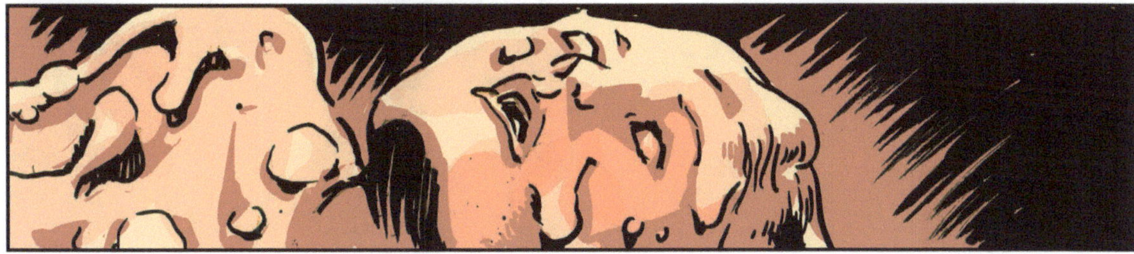

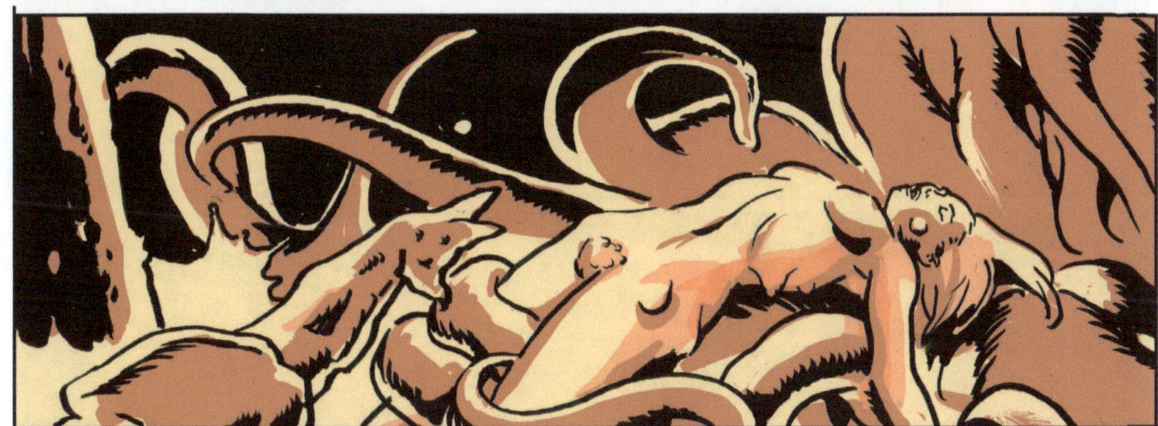

HANG ON, TESS!!!

TESS!

TESS!
CHRIS, WHAT'S GOING ON? WHERE ARE WE? WHAT'S... WHAT'S ALL OVER ME? IT TASTES LIKE...

JUST GET CLEAR OF THIS THING!

CHRIS!
AH! IT'S GOT ME!

TESS! TE....
CHRIS! DON'T LET GO!

CHRIS...

FORBIDDEN FUTURES 13

CHRIS!!
GLUB...

MMMM,
SO GOOD...

CHRIS?

CHRIS!!!

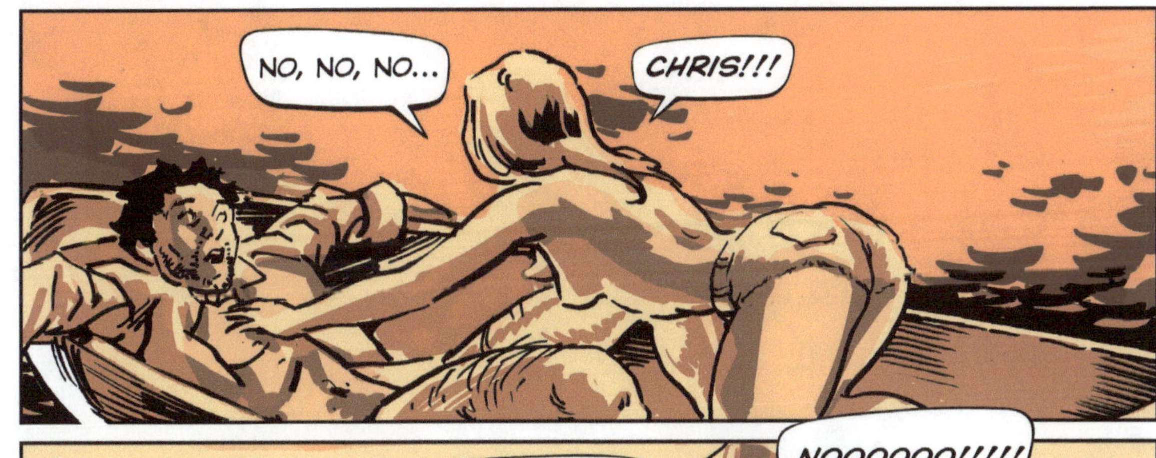

NO, NO, NO...
CHRIS!!!

DON'T DIE ON ME- CHRIS!!!
NOOOOOO!!!!!

AH, SWEET RELEASE! WHEN OFFERED AN OPENING, SOMETIMES YOU CAN'T HELP BUT GO WITH THE FLOW. AFTER ALL, SOME RELATIONSHIPS ARE ALL-CONSUMING- WE KNOW CHRIS AND TESS'S WILL BE.
WELL, I GOTTA GO, I'M FEELING THE CALL! I HOPE YOU ENJOYED THIS SNAPPER OF A SICK STORY! CUM AGAIN!

CREDITS

CHARLIE BRANCH is a libraian from a small Kansas town, who enjoys cats, gardening and the ocassional space opera novel, and has reread Dune ten times.

ERICA L. SATIFKA has appeared in *Apex Magazine, Interzone, Nature,* and many other places. Her debut collection *How to Get To Apocalypse and Other Disasters* (Fairwood Press) was named one of the best SF books of the year by the Washington Post and Locus, and won the 2021 Endeavour Award. She lives in Portland, Oregon.

CODY GOODFELLOW has written nine novels and five collections of short stories. His writing has been favored with three Wonderland Book Awards. His comics work has been featured in *Mystery Meat, Creepy, Slow Death Zero* and *Skin Crawl.* As an actor, he has appeared in numerous short films, TV shows, music videos by Anthrax and Beck, and a Days Inn commercial. He also wrote, co-produced and scored the Lovecraftian hygiene films *Baby Got Bass* and *Stay At Home Dad,* which can be viewed on YouTube. He lives in San Diego, California.

ELIZABETH RAYNE is a she-writer owned by a parrot. When not writing, she can most likely be found cosplaying as a character nobody ever heard of.

PHILIP FRACASSI is the author of the novels *Don't Let Them Get You Down, A Child Alone with Strangers, Gothic,* and *Boys in the Valley.* His upcoming books include the novels *Sarafina* and *The Third Rule of Time Travel.*

MIKE DUBISCH has designed characters and illustrated windows into multiple universes, from *Star Wars* to *Dungeons and Dragons, Aliens VS Predator, The Wheel Of Time,* and the Cthulhu Mythos. With the publisher Oddness, Mike collaborates with the world's greatest genre fiction writers to help create new universes every issue of Forbidden Futures. A veteran of role playing games, underground horror comix, pulp science fiction magazines and role playing game miniatures, Mike has been a professional illustrator for over three decades, and is known as a visionary fantasy illustrator, surrealist and graphic novelist.

SAM RICHARD is the author of *Sabbath of the Fox-Devils* and the Wonderland Award-Winning Collection *To Wallow in Ash & Other Sorrows.* The owner of Weirdpunk Books, he has edited and co-edited several anthologies, including the Splatterpunk Award-Nominated *The New Flesh: A Literary Tribute to David Cronenberg, Zombie Punks Fuck Off,* and *Beautiful/Grotesque.* Widowed in 2017, he slowly rots in Minneapolis with his dog, Nero.

JAN STEVEN STRNAD (sometimes credited as J. Knight) is an American writer of comic books, horror, and science fiction. He is known for his many collaborations with artist Richard Corben, as well as his work in the Star Wars expanded universe, the majority of which has been published by Dark Horse Comics. He has also written for DC Comics, Marvel Comics, Eclipse Comics, and Fantagraphics Books.

ODDNESS (author, publisher, producer) originates from unknown lands, and dabbles in modular synths and playing video games.